Cupcakes and Corruption

The Pupcake Mystery Series Prequel

By Mary B. Barbee

Mystic Valley Press

A Sweet Suggestion

The bittersweet aroma of coffee hung in the air as Eliza Campbell and her husband, Dean, sat across from each other at their kitchen table. Eliza's mousy-brown hair was tied up in a messy bun like most days, stray strands of hair framing her rosy cheeks. Her curtain bangs hung low over her shiny hazel eyes, hiding her thinning eyebrows and a hint of forehead wrinkles and teasing her naturally dark eyelashes with every blink.

Pupcake, Eliza's toy-sized chihuahua and close companion, sat in her lap with his back straight, his big brown eyes not quite level with the top of Eliza's bowl of yogurt in front of her. Eliza mindlessly twirled the ends of Pupcake's ears between her fingers as she stared out the window, ignoring her breakfast. Robins of all sizes hopped around on the dewy grass looking for worms. Pupcake twitched his ear and glanced up at "his person," communicating in his own way with Eliza, letting her know that he'd prefer to be petted differently. She smiled down at him and scratched his head instead. Pupcake let out a sigh of approval and rested his head on Eliza's knee, watching all the happenings out the window.

"Did you read about the baking contest at the county fair, my love?" Dean asked, his chin tilted down as he gazed over his reading glasses at his wife. Dean was three years older than Eliza, his fiftieth birthday right around the corner. His dark hair was starting to show glimmers of gray at his temples, but many might say that he was still handsome and aging gracefully. Eliza often teased her husband about his new salt and pepper hairstyle, but she thought it made him look even more sophisticated than when he was in his younger years.

Eliza was especially grateful for how her husband made his health a priority, and she tried hard to keep up so they could enjoy their lives together for many years to come. Like clockwork, Dean woke up early every weekday morning and went for a swim at the local community center. For years, Eliza had stayed on a strict workout schedule herself, easily running five miles on the treadmill in their sunroom three to four times a week, but her new coffee shop required more of her time than she had originally expected. Now, she couldn't remember the last time she had even tied the laces of her running shoes.

"Umm-uh," Eliza mumbled, as she scooped a spoonful of blueberries and vanilla Greek yogurt into her mouth. She slipped her phone out of her pocket as she chewed and swallowed her bite. She held a finger up in the air as if to ask Dean to give her a minute before speaking again. She opened the reminder app on her iPhone and quickly typed, *Work out*. In seconds, she had assigned tomorrow as the reminder date, locked her screen, and pushed the phone back into her jeans pocket.

Dean seemed to have become accustomed to Eliza's quick note-taking habits since she first started her business, but Eliza made an effort to keep her phone out of sight as much as possible when they were together. Dean was supportive of Eliza's dream to open a coffee shop, and she truly never wanted him to feel neglected due to her demanding schedule.

"Well, it looks like something that's right up your alley," Dean continued when Eliza's phone was back in her pocket and he had her attention again. He folded the paper and pushed it across the table to Eliza. He tapped his finger on the article. "It says there are cash prizes, but for the first time in history, I guess, the winner will also be featured in the *Sugar and Spice* national dessert magazine. That could bring a lot of exposure to the shop." Dean winked at her, and Eliza instinctively grinned. Her husband's winks still triggered butterflies to flutter around in her stomach, although a bit calmer after their twenty-five years together.

Eliza picked up the paper with one hand, the other reaching for another spoonful of yogurt. She was instantly intrigued. Her eyes scanned the words in the newspaper in front of her like a hungry hawk searching for dinner at dusk. Her mind raced with excitement for what it could mean for her new coffee shop, but within seconds, the excitement quickly turned to self-doubt.

"I don't know, the shop has only just opened. " Eliza said, setting the paper back down on the table and pushing it back to Dean. "I'm probably not good enough to win anyway. Plus, I'm already so busy just trying to run the place. I couldn't possibly expect to win, or even find time to *enter* a baking contest right now."

Dean raised his left eyebrow, and Eliza could practically read his mind. Dean knew Eliza better than anyone. It had been just over a year and a half since their youngest child had left for college, and the loneliness had taken its toll on Eliza. Like many mothers, she struggled with empty nest syndrome after her kids moved away to start their own lives. Dean proved to be a wonderfully supportive partner as they navigated their new child-free lives together.

Dean's first attempt to help was to bring home Pupcake, the tiniest puppy either Dean or Eliza had ever seen, at only eight weeks old. Eliza raised her new little puppy from the size of a soup can to the perfect smaller-than-your-lap size, which served well as a temporary distraction and replaced her loneliness with joy. Eliza and Pupcake became inseparable. Wherever Eliza went, you were sure to find Pupcake tucked away in her purse or a backpack, or just propped perfectly in her arms. But sooner than expected, Pupcake was fully trained and needed less and less attention. Pupcake was a smart dog, very quickly mastering all the things a well-mannered puppy should learn, and it wasn't long before Eliza was back to that familiar struggle that she lacked purpose. Eliza found herself looking for a new project.

There were several instances when Dean had expressed concern for Eliza's ability to find a life of her own that didn't involve raising children or puppy training, so with Dean's encouragement, Eliza took the leap and finally fulfilled her lifelong dream of owning a coffee shop. She opened Pupcake's Corner Café, named after the cutest member of the family, of course, and located right at the end of Main Street in Copeland's busiest shopping area.

Pupcake himself joined Eliza at work every day, greeting each customer with an open pup smile and a wag of his tail. She swore Pupcake was a big reason for all the success the café had experienced so far, often hearing how he had created quite the reputation for himself around town.

The café was only one week away from celebrating its third month since its opening, and Eliza was honestly happier than she had been in years.

"Well, if you ask me, I vote that you enter your famous strawberry cupcakes. Everyone is talking about them. Even new clients that come in the firm mention them as soon as they make the connection that I'm married to the owner of the new coffee shop downtown." Dean winked at Eliza again and grinned. The butterflies in her stomach fluttered about as Eliza locked eyes with her husband. She knew he was so proud of her, and it felt amazing.

Eliza returned the smile. "Well, I'll think about it. It's true that they're my most popular item." She picked up Pupcake and buried her nose in his scruff, making kissing sounds as she nuzzled next to his ear. Stuffing him under her arm in a football hold, she stood up and carried her bowl and spoon with her free hand to the sink.

She glanced at the clock on the wall. "Speaking of the shop, I need to get going. Do you have time…"

"I've got this," Dean answered her question before she finished her sentence. He snuck a short little kiss on the top of Pupcake's head and gently nudged the two of them out of the way. He began rinsing the dishes and stacking them strategically in the empty dishwasher.

Eliza set Pupcake carefully on the floor and opened the back door for him to go potty. She turned and wrapped her arms around Dean from behind, lifting her head to place a kiss on the nape of his neck.

"I really hit the jackpot with you, my love. Thank you so much for being so wonderful." She stood on her toes and leaned in to give him a quick kiss on the cheek.

Dean turned around, quickly wiping his hands on a towel before embracing her. He pulled his wife in close as he leaned back against the counter, pushing his lips against hers. Eliza melted in his arms, welcoming the kiss that she knew was meant to last her all day.

"It's truly easy," Dean brushed Eliza's bangs out of her eyes. He smiled a close-lipped smile and dropped his arms down, lightly placing his hands on her hips.

"Now go and sell lots of delicious goodies. See you at dinner," he said before turning his attention back to the dishes.

"Thanks, honey." Eliza turned to leave.

"Come on, little guy," she said to Pupcake, who had returned from outside and was waiting patiently at Eliza's feet. He was resting on his hind legs, his left back foot lifted slightly off the ground. Eliza wasn't sure what inspired that little signal, but she recognized it as Pupcake's way of communicating that he wanted to be held. She bent down and scooped him up, one hand under his belly. Tucking him under her arm again, she grabbed the fabric sling Pupcake liked so much, her purse, and her car keys.

"Have a good day, honey! See you tonight!" Eliza said as she headed out the door.

She had driven about a mile down the road, with Pupcake clicked into his car-safe carrier in the seat next to her when she realized she was still smiling.

Quite the Commotion

Eliza parked her car and watched as her only employee, Taylor Turnbull, stepped off her bike and removed her helmet. Taylor tipped her chin up and shook her head, quickly running a hand through her shoulder-length blond hair.

"Good morning, Taylor!" Eliza called out, fumbling in her purse for the keys to the back door of the shop. She unclicked Pupcake from his seat and held out his sling. He stepped in and settled right down, his big brown eyes watching Eliza's every move as she stood and slipped the sling over her head.

"Good morning, Eliza!" Taylor responded cheerily. "Another day, another dollar, right?" Her bright smile was genuine and infectious.

Eliza chuckled. One of the things she loved about Taylor was her positive attitude. When Eliza first met Taylor, she wondered if Taylor's bubbly personality was just a show for the interview, but as it turned out, she was an authentically happy and positive person all the time. Sometimes she could be a bit chatty for Eliza's taste, but most of the time, Eliza appreciated Taylor's energy. And the customers seemed to feel comfortable with her. That was the most important thing to Eliza, considering her business was so new to Copeland.

Watching as Taylor latched her bike lock around the loosely attached gutter that ran along the cement wall that was the back of the shop, Eliza's motherly instincts kicked in. She couldn't help but suggest to Taylor to use the bike rack in front of the shop instead.

"I'm not sure that gutter is going to do much for security back here," Eliza called out, gesturing to the flimsy gutter.

Taylor smiled and shrugged her shoulders, her hands on her hips and her helmet hooked on her thumb. "Thanks, but I'm not worried about it. Besides, my mom was telling me she read that Copeland's property theft ratings had dropped quite a bit lately with the new chief of police in town."

"Well, that's definitely good to hear." Eliza adjusted Pupcake's sling to make room on her shoulder for her purse strap.

Eliza had spent her entire life in the southern city of Copeland, and she couldn't imagine living anywhere else despite the crime uptick in the past few years. It had always been such a peaceful small town, and she was relieved that the new chief of police was making positive changes.

She approached the back door of the shop and slipped the key into the lock. Leaning back slightly as she always did when she unlocked the heavy door, she pulled the door handle. She almost lost her balance when the door opened before she even turned the key.

"Whoa," Eliza said. "The door wasn't locked."

Eliza used her free shoulder to hold the heavy door open. She slid the large rock she kept just outside the door jamb to prop the door open as she and Taylor stepped inside the storage room. The beams of sunlight streaming in from outside cast eerie shadows on the shelves of baking supplies. Eliza swatted at the dust floating in the air.

She reached over and switched on the lights before turning her attention to the alarm keypad on the wall. It was beeping quietly, counting down the two minutes it allowed for Eliza to punch in the alarm code as she entered.

"Well, at least the alarm was set," she said, breathing a sigh of relief. "Stay here, though. I'll check to make sure everything is okay," Eliza told Taylor before walking through the storage room into the kitchen and then the dining room. As far as she could tell, everything was in order.

Returning to find Taylor still standing by the back door, Eliza shrugged her shoulders.

"Everything is fine," Eliza tried to ignore the nagging uneasiness that she was experiencing, realizing that she may have forgotten to lock the back door to her new shop.

"Weird," Taylor said, sounding unconcerned.

"Yeah, I don't know…" Eliza's words trailed off, shaking her head as she subconsciously petted Pupcake under the chin.

Taylor stowed her purse in her assigned locker, and Eliza followed suit. Taylor walked past Eliza, humming quietly, and grabbed a clean apron from the hooks on the wall beside the door of the walk-in cooler.

"Are you okay?" Taylor asked Eliza, as she reached over and gave Pupcake a little scratch behind the ears.

"Oh yeah, I'm fine," Eliza responded, having already decided she would add a reminder note to the door so that never happened again.

"Okay, good," Then turning her attention to Pupcake, "You look sleepy, little man," Taylor said to Pupcake.

"Me, too," Taylor continued. "I need to start going to bed earlier. I live so close to here that I keep justifying hitting the snooze button every morning. Then, I inevitably end up rushing out the door half asleep."

"You sound like my daughter, Laura. It almost seemed like a personal challenge for her to get as much sleep in as possible before having to face the day." Eliza smiled, relieved to be distracted from the unlocked door. She sighed quietly. She missed seeing her daughter every morning, and she was just now realizing how working with Taylor had somehow contributed to filling that void.

Taylor laughed and nodded. "Yep, one hundred percent. That's my daily challenge, too."

Pupcake yawned and stretched his neck. Eliza pulled him out of his sling, gave him a little hug, and set him down on the floor, closing the heavy door shut behind her and locking it.

"Should I start some coffee?" Taylor asked as she wrapped the apron strings around her tiny waist twice, tying them in a neat little bow in the front.

"That sounds perfect. I'll set up Pupcake's little space and preheat the oven for the cinnamon rolls. I made them up last night and set them in the refrigerator to save a bit of time this morning. I've been wanting to try this new trick I just read about in the *Sugar and Spice* magazine. It was all about baking the perfect prepped-ahead-of-time cinnamon rolls. The article said now that I've prepared them, I just need to pop the refrigerated rolls in the oven while it preheats and then bake them the normal amount of time."

Eliza reached for a clean apron and tucked her head through the neck hole.

"So, we'll see how they turn out, I guess!"

"I would be honored to be the taste tester," Taylor called out as she made her way to the other side of the shop where four coffee pots sat side-by-side on a counter along the wall. "I happen to know a thing or two about delicious cinnamon rolls."

"Done! You are now my official taste tester," Eliza teased. "I may need to change your title in my records, though," she chuckled.

After setting the oven to preheat and slipping the pan of cinnamon rolls inside, Eliza pulled Pupcake's bed and blanket out from where it was stowed under the front counter. She set up his little station in the front corner of the dining room, right in front of the picture windows, where he could nap or lay and enjoy a sidewalk view.

Pupcake was always such a good boy. Eliza joked that he was actually more of a person than a dog. He rarely barked at anything, and he was easily everyone's best friend. When Eliza first brought Pupcake to the shop and let him wander around, she worried that Pupcake would get stepped on by someone since he was so little, but he did a fantastic job at taking care of himself, expertly dodging feet whenever needed. She no longer worried about that at all, and the customers loved visiting with Pupcake just as much as he loved the attention. She knew for a fact that there were a few customers who returned week after week just to see Pupcake, and she was okay with that, especially when they also bought coffee or food during their visit.

"Coffee is ready!" Taylor called out, pouring two cups and adding sugar and cream to both.

"Yum! I'll be right there," Eliza responded, coaxing Pupcake over to show him where she had set up his spot. He stood on top of his bed, kicking his front and back legs out alternatively while turning a circle to form a perfect little round nest. He yawned and settled down for an early morning nap.

"You're a good boy, Pupcake." She stroked the tiny dog's soft golden brown fur.

Eliza stood and tidied up the little bookshelf next to Pupcake's spot. Picturebooks, magazines and puzzle books for all different ages sat on the top two shelves, and the bottom two shelves contained a small selection of fun classic board games. She straightened out the fairy string lights that draped along the top shelf and stretched out over the front window.

She turned and looked around, surveying her shop's quaint little dining area. Six small round tables were placed just the right space apart in the center of the room, providing the perfect blend of a cozy and private ambiance. Small vases decorated each table which she filled every morning with one fresh flower from the flower shop next door. A long high table was pushed up to the front window. Comfortable bar stools with soft royal blue cushions were lined up neatly and pushed under the table.

When Eliza felt like the dining room was in order, she joined Taylor behind the counter and thanked her for the coffee.

"You're welcome! I tried to make it just as you like it. Two sugar cubes and one dollop of cream, right?" Taylor asked.

Eliza nodded and took a sip. "It's perfect," she said, her lips pressed into a small smile.

Taylor grinned, lifting her cup to her lips.

"So, besides the cinnamon rolls, are we cooking anything else this morning?" Taylor asked between sips of her coffee.

"Yeah, I want to make a couple of peaches and cream pies this morning and test how they do. It doesn't require any baking, but there are still a few steps involved. Have you ever made anything like that?"

"No, but I'm excited to learn something new," Taylor said enthusiastically, setting her coffee down.

"I love that." A warm smile spread across Eliza's face.

"I bought some fresh peaches at the farmers' market, so let's start by peeling them. Follow me, I'll show you a little trick I know." Eliza turned to head into the kitchen and she motioned for Taylor to follow her.

She grabbed a large pot and began filling it with warm water. "If you immerse the peaches in boiling water for something like 45 seconds, you can just pinch the skin and pull it all off at once. No knife needed."

"Oh, cool!" Taylor exclaimed, "I totally want to try that."

The oven's timer chimed to announce the preheating session was concluded. Eliza grabbed her phone out of her pocket and set the timer for the cinnamon rolls to finish baking. Learning from past mistakes, she made sure to label the timer *Cinnamon Rolls*. She grabbed the peaches from the shelf and began to gather the rest of the ingredients for the pies.

"I'll make the graham cracker crusts if you want to work on softening the cream cheese in the microwave and prepping the whipped cream. Here are the recipe details." Eliza set the piece of paper on the stainless steel counter next to all the ingredients.

"I'm on it," Taylor said, opening the package of cream cheese while her eyes scanned the recipe.

A loud bang on the front door caused Eliza's heart to jump in her throat and she let out a short screech. Loud high-pitched barking ensued from Pupcake's corner of the store.

"What was that?" Taylor asked urgently.

Eliza leaned forward to be able to look around the wall and see the front door. No one was there.

"I'm not sure," Eliza said. "It sounded like someone hit the door, didn't it?"

"Yeah." Taylor, now standing directly next to Eliza, held her hand tight onto Eliza's upper arm. "That scared me to death. Do you see anyone?"

"No, I don't see anyone." Eliza leaned forward, trying to get a better view.

Pupcake's barking had manifested into a growl, and the hair on Eliza's neck stood on end.

"Stay here," Eliza said for the second time that morning, "I'm going to go check."

Taylor released her grip on her arm and nodded.

Eliza threw her shoulders back and headed toward the door, hoping that the confident posture would have a positive effect on her actual confidence level. She approached the door and without unlocking it, she looked both directions up and down the street. A few cars were parked along Main Street, but there wasn't a soul walking around outside. A black cat cried out and sped across the street away from her building. Eliza leaned closer to the window so much so that her nose touched the glass, hoping to get an even better view. She thought she saw a flash of movement at the end of the block, but she couldn't be sure it was anything at all. She had a moment where she wondered if her mind was playing tricks on her, but she remembered Taylor heard the sound, too.

She stepped back and inspected the glass of the door and the large floor-to-ceiling window. Everything was intact.

"It's all clear!" Eliza called out to Taylor. "Must've been a bird or something."

Taylor peeked around the wall. "Well, *that* will wake you up," she chuckled before returning to her station.

Pupcake settled back down in his bed as if that was all the reassurance he needed, as well.

Eliza's phone chimed. She pulled it out of her pocket to find that she had a new text message from Laura: *Dad messaged me and Dalton about the contest. He's right - your cupcakes will totally win, Mom!*

Eliza rolled her eyes, but a huge smile spread across her face. With all the stress she had been experiencing since she arrived that morning, she had not spent another minute thinking about the contest. But, she loved hearing from her daughter, and the text message instantly put her back at ease.

She locked her phone screen, slipped it back into her pocket and returned to the kitchen. She took another sip of her coffee. Leaning against the counter, her arms crossed and her coffee mug in hand, she took a deep breath and exhaled slowly.

"Alright, how are you doing, Taylor? Do you need anything?"

Taylor shook her head. "Nope, the cream cheese is ready and I'm almost finished with the whipped cream. I'll move on to the peaches next."

"Wonderful," Eliza said. "I'll get on those crusts and then stock the cases out front."

A few minutes after she began to get lost in her tasks, her phone chimed again. It was the alarm letting her know that it was time to check the cinnamon rolls. Peeking inside the oven, Eliza was pleased to see the sweet rolls had risen a bit and turned a golden brown.

"They look perfect!" Eliza set the hot pan on the cooling rack next to the stovetop. Within minutes, she was able to push the unlocked door and the strange noise out of her mind and lose herself in the work that she loved dearly.

The Morning Rush

E liza flipped the closed sign on the front door of the Pupcake Corner Cafe' to read "*Open*" right on time and returned to the kitchen to check on the peaches and cream pies Taylor had finished and placed in the cooler. The pies needed a bit more time to solidify, and Eliza decided they would have to either be introduced as an afternoon treat or wait to be served until the next day.

Just minutes later, the bell chimed on the front door. She greeted her first few customers of the day with a smile and a warm, "Welcome!" Mrs. Wilson was one of her very favorite customers and was almost always first in line. Eliza had memorized Mrs. Wilson's order since she always ordered the same thing: a chai latte with soy milk, and a cheese danish.

Pupcake sat quietly on his hind legs by the pastry case at the front of the line as if petting him was officially part of the ordering process.

After greeting Pupcake with lots of scratches behind the ears, Mrs. Wilson shifted her focus to Eliza, "Did you read the paper this morning? It's time for the county fair's annual baking contest again. You *have* to enter!"

Mrs. Wilson was in her mid-sixties, looked to be in excellent athletic shape for her age, and had a headful of feathery gray hair cut short and close. She adored Eliza, Pupcake, and the café. She was very active at the local tennis club, and Eliza had heard that she insisted to everyone she knew there that they visit the café. Eliza was very grateful for the support and always offered for Mrs. Wilson's order to be free as a way to show her appreciation, but Mrs. Wilson would never hear of it.

"Yes, ma'am. I saw that. My husband, Dean, said the same thing when he saw the article." Eliza grinned as she placed a lid on the disposable cup. "I promised I would give it some thought."

Taylor handed Mrs. Wilson a small blue-striped cardboard box with the danish tucked inside. A piece of twine was tied around the box and into a bow, and Taylor had written Mrs. Wilson's name on the top with one of the shop's many blue markers found under the counter. Eliza was particular about the packaging at her café and she appreciated Taylor's efforts to follow her instructions to a tee.

"Let me give this one to you on the house, Mrs. Wilson," Eliza pleaded. Mrs. Wilson shook her head emphatically.

"How are you supposed to stay open if you give away your delicious food and drinks all the time?" Mrs. Wilson asked as she pushed a five-dollar bill towards Eliza and dropped a few folded-up one-dollar bills into the tip jar sitting next to the cash register.

"Thank you so much, Mrs. Wilson." Eliza smiled warmly. Five dollars didn't cover the cost of the latte and the danish, so at least she felt better about her best customer getting a discount.

"Have a wonderful day today!" Taylor called out, cheerily.

"Oh, I'm not leaving yet. I want to talk to Eliza more about the contest." Mrs. Wilson responded with a grin and a wink. A line had formed behind the "order here" sign, so she stepped to the other side of Pupcake to patiently wait to talk to Eliza more as she worked. Eliza greeted the next customer, a strawberry blonde-haired lady that looked about the same age as herself, and maybe a few years younger. She began to prepare her Americano as Taylor grabbed a cinnamon roll and placed it on a small porcelain white plate with a dainty light blue and gold trimmed edge.

The customer smiled at Mrs. Wilson. "I couldn't help but overhear y'all talking about the contest at the fair. I, one hundred percent, agree you should enter, Eliza. Your treats are so good!"

Mrs. Wilson nodded emphatically after a sip from her to-go cup.

"That's what I was telling her! She would definitely win!"

Then, a third lady a few places further in line chimed in, "And it would be good to have a different winner for a change, let me tell you. That lady who owns the bakery on 5th, Margaret Minks, wins every single year. She enters the same apple pie every year, and every year I think there's no way she'll win again. Some people think she pays off the judges."

Taylor whispered to Eliza that she needed to excuse herself to the bathroom. Eliza nodded and asked her to hurry back.

Mrs. Wilson leaned over the counter and crooked her finger motioning for Eliza to come closer. Eliza looked at the line in front of her and told the next customer, "I'll be right back." She walked a few steps closer to where Mrs. Wilson stood on the other side of the pastry case and leaned in so that their faces were only inches apart.

"What's happening?" Eliza whispered. She spotted Pupcake looking up at her from where he sat next to Mrs. Wilson's feet.

"Do you know who Taylor is?" Mrs. Wilson asked.

"What do you mean?" Eliza was impatient but tried not to show it.

"You should ask her how she knows Margaret Minks," Mrs. Wilson whispered before pulling away.

Eliza held Mrs. Wilson's gaze for a few seconds before realizing she wasn't going to say anything further.

"Okay," Eliza said, the intonation of the word sounding more like a question than a confirmation. She was confused, but she didn't have time for the small-town gossip when the line to order was stretched throughout the dining area. She turned back to the next customer and began making his white chocolate mocha.

The chatter continued between a few of the ladies in line and those who chose dining seats close by. Eliza could only pick up bits and pieces of the conversation as she continued to work, but there was much debate over whether Margaret Minks, the owner of the bakery on Fifth Avenue, had won the last several baking contests fairly or not.

The door chimed again as a lady wearing a large-brimmed straw hat and dark sunglasses made a quick exit. Eliza pushed away the touch of anxiety that surfaced for just a moment as she wondered if the lady was impatient. The line was quite long, and Eliza was moving as quickly as she could.

Where in the world is Taylor, Eliza thought to herself. She glanced back through the kitchen, but Taylor was not in sight, and the bathroom door was still closed.

The next customer in line seemed familiar to Eliza, but she didn't know her name.

"Hi, there!" Eliza smiled. "What can I get for you today?"

"I want a couple of those strawberry cupcakes. Hon, I honestly think you should enter those cupcakes in that baking contest. They are to die for and would no doubt win the prize."

Eliza smiled and raised her eyebrows. There certainly were a lot of opinions about her entering the contest. *Too bad it isn't a popularity contest*, she thought to herself.

"Well, that is almost exactly what my husband said this morning. I'll have to give it some thought, for sure. Thank you so much for your support! I don't believe we've met yet. May I please ask your name?" Eliza stood poised, sharpie in hand, ready to write the customer's name on the cup.

"Oh, it's Stefanie, spelled with an F." She flashed a bright white smile at Eliza with a wink. "I've been in here before, but it's always so busy. It's good to officially meet you. I love your café, and your dog is just the cutest!"

Eliza beamed. "Thank you," she said graciously, carefully writing Stefanie's name on the cup. "Pupcake is a pretty special little guy, and we are enjoying running the café. Everyone is so kind." She paused before continuing, glancing at the long line of smiling faces, "...and patient, too! I wish I had more time to get to know everyone."

Taylor finally returned from the bathroom after what seemed like an eternity. She looked to be surveying the dining room as she washed her hands in the small sink behind the counter. Within minutes, she jumped right back in and began helping with packaging goodies and making coffee drinks.

It took a little over two hours for the morning rush to end. Eliza was filled with a mixture of exhaustion and exhilaration.

"Whew!" She turned to Taylor. "That was something else!"

"Yes ma'am," Taylor said. "I think we're getting even busier."

Eliza nodded as she silently counted the tips. She pulled a pad of paper out from under the cash register and jotted down the total before opening the cash drawer and slipping it all into the deposit bag labeled *Cash Tips*. So many of the tips were run electronically, so Eliza had taken her accountant's advice and just added Taylor's share to her paycheck instead of giving her cash each day.

Taylor headed into the kitchen to wash some dishes before her shift ended. Eliza only had Taylor on the payroll during the busiest morning shifts. So far, she could easily handle the lunch and afternoon shifts on her own.

Eliza's mind was racing from all the talk about the contest, but she also couldn't shake the sight of the woman who had left so quickly without ordering. Eliza couldn't recall that ever happening before, and she was definitely taking it personally. She was frustrated that she didn't even get a good look at the customer to recognize her if she ever came in again.

She grabbed a cleaning rag from behind the counter and began mindlessly wiping off surfaces around her. She would have to let that go. It could've been anything. After all, the customer may have received an urgent personal text message and may have had to leave in a hurry to deal with that.

Eliza shifted her attention to the dining room. A young couple was sitting in front of the window finishing their coffees. They were sitting close together, and he had one hand on her knee. The young girl threw her head back when she laughed, and Eliza thought the young man's face almost glowed each time she did so.

At a table a few feet away from them was a younger man sitting alone, his laptop computer open on the table in front of him. His serious expression and level of concentration gave Eliza the impression that he must be working on some sort of project.

She wiped off the empty tables and checked on the couple to see if they needed anything. She decided not to disturb the man with the computer. Pupcake was sound asleep in his bed by the window.

Eliza glanced at her watch. She had just enough time to restock the pastry case and supplies and make another pot of regular coffee before lunch. While she was making the coffee, she decided to pour herself a cup of Double Bergamot Earl Grey tea, as well.

Taylor poked her head around the wall from the kitchen.

"I'm headed out, Eliza," she said, "unless you need something else before I go?"

Eliza shook her head. "No, I'm good. Thanks so much for all your hard work again today, Taylor!"

"Of course!" She smiled, as she pulled her apron over her head.

Eliza watched as the couple set their plates on the dirty dishes station and hugged each other goodbye. The girl turned and called out "Thank you!" with a wave of her hand as they exited the store.

Eliza called back, "Come back soon!" Both patrons nodded and assured Eliza they would.

Turning her attention back to Taylor, who had bent down to scratch Pupcake behind the ears and whispered that she would see him tomorrow, as if it was their little secret.

"Be safe getting home, and I'll see you tomorrow morning!"

"Yep, I'll be here," Taylor called over her shoulder as she started her way toward the back door. "I can't wait to try that peaches and cream pie."

"Oh! I almost forgot!" Eliza exclaimed, setting her tea down, and following Taylor towards the back of the store to check on the pies.

Taylor had one hand on the door when Eliza suddenly remembered what Mrs. Wilson said to her.

"Oh! Taylor, one more thing." Eliza stood with the heavy door of the cooler open.

Taylor stopped and turned back to look at Eliza.

"Hmm?"

"Something that Mrs. Wilson said today..." Eliza began.

Taylor shifted her weight and looked down at the floor.

"Do you know Margaret Minks? The one who owns the bakery on Fifth Avenue?" Eliza asked.

Taylor looked up at Eliza, her nose wrinkled as if she caught a sniff of something awful.

"Yeah," Taylor responded. "I know her."

Taylor paused before continuing. Eliza couldn't be sure, but she thought Taylor's eyes appeared almost apologetic.

"She's my mom's sister. Margaret is my aunt."

Friendship Friction

E liza turned left into her subdivision. Pupcake sat quietly in his safety carrier, happy as a clam to just look out the window.

"I'm so sorry, Susan. I know. I've been so busy with the shop. I just haven't even had a minute to get back to you." Eliza was talking on the phone to her best friend of over fifteen years.

"Seriously? You can't even respond to a text message, Eliza?" Susan asked, the irritation clear in her voice. "I'm starting to feel like you're avoiding me or something."

"I promise, Susan. It's not like that. I'm just so busy during the day and then exhausted at night." Eliza rolled her eyes, which is something she would never do if the two women were sitting across from each other face-to-face. She hadn't been purposefully avoiding Susan, but it was because of conversations like this that Eliza almost dreaded talking to her lately. She reached over to pet Pupcake with her right hand, her left hand remaining on the steering wheel.

Susan and Eliza first met when their children were very young. The two mothers shared so many playdates, were room mothers together, planned birthday parties together, and so much more. When the youngest of their children graduated from high school and went off to college, the pair leaned on each other to get through the sadness and emptiness that followed.

However, Eliza had decided to pursue her dreams and open Pupcake's Corner Cafe.

Susan continued to search for a hobby or a passion that would distract her, and she felt exceptionally lonely without Eliza to talk to each and every day. On the one hand, Eliza understood Susan's feelings, but on the other hand, she wasn't getting any support from Susan. Susan had only visited the shop one time in the last few months that it had been open, and she would quickly change the subject anytime Eliza would talk about it. The relationship between the two friends was definitely strained.

"Why don't you and Jason come over for dinner and dominoes this weekend, Susan? It'll be just like it used to be," Eliza hoped that they could have a conversation and resolve things.

"I'll check with Jason," Susan said, sounding a bit short. "He's not really wanting anything to do with me lately, though."

Susan could be dramatic, so Eliza put little weight into that comment. "Well, he has always enjoyed our game nights. Tell him that Dean will make his favorite barbecued chicken on the grill."

"Yeah. It does sound like fun," Susan mumbled. "I miss you, Eliza."

Eliza wondered if Susan was about to cry. "I miss you, too, Sue. Is everything ok?" She almost cringed as she asked the question. She wasn't lying when she said she was busy. Her plate was full, and she wasn't sure if she had anything left to give to anyone, her best friend included.

Susan paused before she responded, "Jason and I are just not happy together anymore. We're going to counseling, and I'm optimistic that everything will be fine. I mean, we've been together over twenty years."

Pupcake let out a tiny growl as they drove past a man walking a tall poodle and glanced back at Eliza almost as if to ask her, *Did you see them?*

"Oh, I'm sorry to hear that," Eliza said sincerely, petting Pupcake on the head with her free hand. "It's tough on couples after the kids go off to college, but you two are strong. I'm sure you'll get through this."

She pulled into the driveway and clicked the button on the remote control positioned on her visor to open the garage door. Pupcake sat tall in his bed, his ears perked. As much as he loves to go everywhere with Eliza, he was always excited to be home.

"Thank you for saying that, Eliza. I think so too." Eliza truly hoped her friend believed that.

"Well, I guess I should let you go. I'll ask Jason about Saturday night and let you know." Susan paused before continuing, "Thank you for taking the time to chat with me."

Eliza thought Susan's last comment sounded a bit sarcastic, but she decided to ignore it, if it was. "It's been great to talk to you. You should come by the shop sometime after the morning rush. I'll buy you a coffee and a pastry."

"Yeah, I'll do that," Susan replied, and Eliza thought she sounded sincere.

Parking her car slowly, Eliza told her friend she'd see her soon and hung up. She gathered Pupcake into one arm and grabbed her purse and his sling in the other as she climbed out of the car.

Walking into the house, Eliza set Pupcake down and opened the back door, watching as he ran outside to chase a squirrel up a tree before going potty.

Leaving the door open, Eliza settled down at the table, laptop in front of her. She typed *Stillson County Fair* into Google's search box and clicked on the link to their website. Front and center on the homepage for the fair was a button to click to join this year's *Sugar & Spice Baking Competition*. She took a deep breath as she completed the intent form and clicked the submit button.

Pupcake had returned from outside, his front paws propped up on the side of her chair, his shiny brown eyes asking to sit in Eliza's lap. She reached down and scooped him up, and he thanked her with a few quick kisses, propped up in front of her, front paws on her chest.

"Well, I did it, Pupcake," Eliza stroked the pup's cheek. He stretched into her pets and went in for another kiss, licking her on the chin.

"Okay, lover boy, I get it... you approve." Eliza giggled. "I wonder if they let dogs attend the fair..."

Pupcake gave a full body shake, starting at his head and vibrating down to the tip of his tail and settled down in her lap, shifting his attention to the backyard.

Eliza picked up her phone and started a group text with Dean and the kids to tell them the news that she officially entered the baking contest.

She was a little nervous, but she thought, *what could she lose?*

The Threat

Eliza awoke to the sound of her cell phone ringing. Thinking it was the alarm, she reached up to the headboard and hit the snooze button on her alarm clock. The ringing stopped.

She glanced over at Pupcake's doggy playpen where he slept, set in front of the nightstand. He laid still as a mouse, on top of his fluffy super-soft white blanket. Looking past Dean and toward the window, she could see only dim light streaming in through the crack between the blinds and the window frame. She reached for her phone on the headboard to check the time.

As soon as she picked up the phone, it began to ring again. A bit more awake this time, she could see it was a phone call coming in from an unknown, but local, phone number. Groggy and confused, she answered with her heart in her throat, immediately scared that one of her kids was in trouble.

"Hello, is this Eliza Campbell?" the man's gruff voice spoke before she did.

"Yes, this is Eliza," she answered. Dean lifted his head, wakened by the sound of concern in his wife's voice, and sat straight up in bed waiting patiently to hear what was happening. He reached out and gently held Eliza's hand, as she met his gaze with worry in her eyes. Dean mouthed the words, *It's* okay, and sat patiently as Eliza returned her attention to the man on the other line.

"Ma'am, I'm sorry to wake you, but there has been a break-in at your coffee shop on Main Street."

Eliza gasped and quietly told Dean, "The coffee shop. There was a break-in."

Dean's eyes widened with concern, and he squeezed Eliza's hand.

The man on the phone continued to explain that he was a police officer who had responded to the alarm just minutes before.

"I'll be right there," Eliza responded, feeling torn. On the one hand, she was relieved that the emergency wasn't about her children at all, but she was, of course, concerned about the damage at the shop. She ended the phone conversation politely and stood to get dressed.

"I'm coming with you," said Dean.

Eliza knew better than to try to convince him otherwise. Dean was a personal injury attorney and her overprotective husband. She knew he was coming with her before the words escaped his lips.

Pupcake stretched his neck and blinked his eyes, just waking up and sensing that something stressful was happening. His tail wagged as Eliza lifted him out of his playpen and set him on the bed.

"Okay, let's get ready then, and once Pupcake goes potty, we can head out."

She rushed to the bathroom and threw her hair into a high ponytail, brushing her teeth and skipping the eye makeup. Dean had thrown on jeans and a t-shirt and was already in the kitchen with Pupcake in the backyard by the time she entered the room.

"Do you want me to pull together a quick cup of tea to go?" Dean asked.

Eliza shook her head. "No, thank you, dear. I don't want to keep the officer waiting."

Pupcake came running into the house when he heard Eliza's voice. He sat at her feet, with his back foot lifted off the floor.

"Yes, you're coming, too," Eliza said under her breath, bending over to pick up the cute little pup. As the three of them made their way out the door and into the car, Eliza received a notification.

Work out, her phone screen read. She swiped left on the notification to clear the screen. *Not today,* she thought to herself.

Eliza, Dean and Pupcake met the police officer at the shop within just twenty minutes of the phone call. The front window had a gaping hole in it. The back door had been forced open by the police to inspect the inside for intruders.

Everything seemed in order. Eliza was relieved to find that nothing was missing or damaged except for the front window. A generic red brick lay on the black and white tile near one of the round tables and a handwritten note was tied to it with twine. The note read: *Stay out of the contest or you'll regret it.*

A shudder ran down Eliza's spine. The paper that the note was written on was thin and glossy. The letters were written carefully with a blue pen.

Once Eliza informed the officer that she just entered the Stillson County Fair's baking contest, he asked Eliza the obvious question. "Do you have any idea who would want you out of the contest?"

Eliza stammered, "Um...no...no, I don't know anyone who would do this." She looked at Dean with tears in her eyes.

Dean reached over and hugged her. "It's ok, honey. We'll fix the window and find out who did this."

Pupcake stretched his neck out of the sling and licked Eliza's cheek as if to say he agreed with Dean. She petted the fur on the back of his neck mindlessly as she stood there, staring at the broken window. Her mind raced, trying to figure out who would do such a terrible thing to her beautiful coffee shop.

She couldn't think of one single suspect.

An Unwelcome Visitor

A few days had passed since Pupcake's Corner Café had been vandalized. The window was replaced, and returning to the busy mornings preparing coffee and pastries for her regular customers proved to be the best way for Eliza to move forward and put it all behind her.

The shop had only closed for one day for repairs, but word had spread around town and even more customers were coming out to show their support. Eliza wouldn't be able to continue much longer without hiring more help to keep up with the crowd. Taylor was a wonderful help, but even the two of them struggled to keep up with the line that formed out the door and down the street each morning. Eliza recognized this was a good problem to have so early in business, but she made a mental note to further assess the situation sooner rather than later.

Once again, the morning rush had passed and the quiet hour had arrived. Taylor had headed home for the day, and only one or two customers remained in the shop. Eliza topped off Pupcake's water bowl with fresh, filtered water before she began wiping off the tables.

The door chime rang out, and Eliza looked up to greet the new customer, an older lady whom Eliza guessed was in her early sixties. Her hair was white and cut in a bob. Her face was thin, her wrinkles showed through a thick layer of poorly applied make-up. Her nose was long and pointed, her jaw square, Eliza thought she looked familiar, but she couldn't be sure and certainly didn't know her name.

"Hi! Welcome!" Eliza called out as she took her spot behind the counter. "How can I help you today?"

The woman seemed a bit standoffish, her face vacant of any kind of smile at all.

"I'll have a cappuccino and one of those strawberry cream cheese cupcakes to go," she said, with an agitated tone.

"Great!" Eliza responded, ignoring the attitude, and began to prepare the customer's coffee drink. After placing the lid on the drink, she opened the case and selected one of the popular cupcakes, placing it on a small sheet of parchment paper just inside the blue-striped cardboard box. She wrapped a piece of twine around the box and tied her signature small bow at the top.

"My name is Margaret Minks, by the way," the woman spoke, never taking her eyes off Eliza's movements. "Do you know who I am?"

Eliza stopped in her tracks. "Why, yes, I think so. You own the bakery on 5th Avenue, right?"

Margaret met her eyes and nodded. "Yep, and I'm also the annual winner of the Stillson County Fair baking contest. For seven years running now."

"Oh." That one word was all Eliza could mutter.

Was this woman responsible for breaking her window? Her mind began racing as she remembered how Taylor had kept the secret from her about her relationship with Ms. Minks. Taylor had explained that she had kept the secret about her relationship with Margaret Minks because she wasn't sure if Eliza would be concerned about Taylor being related to the owner of a competing bakery. This explanation made good sense to Eliza and now, meeting Ms. Minks for the first time, she could see why Taylor - having such a positive attitude - would not enjoy working with her aunt.

But, she was also known to be too trusting. Laura would often tell her that not everyone deserves the benefit of the doubt, despite Eliza's general faith in people.

Could the two of them be working together to sabotage her shop? Eliza certainly wasn't brave enough to come right out and accuse Ms. Minks of the vandalism, so she chose to focus on Margaret's order and keep the conversation as light as possible.

Pupcake sauntered over to Ms. Minks and began sniffing her shoes. He exhaled a quick loud breath of air, sounding a bit like a disapproving snort, before walking away with his nose in the air.

Eliza stifled a chuckle. She knew from experience that Pupcake was a good judge of character.

Ms. Minks didn't seem to notice Pupcake by her feet at all, or if she did, she didn't acknowledge him.

"So, this is the cupcake you're entering in the contest, I understand." Margaret stood tall and fearless.

"Yes, that is correct." Eliza hated how weak her voice sounded.

"Well, I just hope you have a thick skin because you don't have any chance of winning. As I said, my apple pie has won the blue ribbon every year for seven years. It's pretty much a waste of time for you to enter, especially with strawberry cream cheese cupcakes." Margaret uttered those last few words as if the concept of strawberry cream cheese cupcakes was just ridiculous.

"Ok. Thank you for the warning," Eliza responded. Looking around, she realized that the shop was empty except for the two of them. "Maybe you should try the cupcakes before you jump to any conclusions, but I'm sure your apple pie is fantastic."

"How much do I owe you?" Margaret asked, ignoring Eliza's suggestion. She had clearly said what she wanted to say and was ready to leave.

"There's no charge today," answered Eliza with a kind smile. "Thank you for stopping by."

Margaret stared at her silently for what seemed like an eternity before giving her one quick nod, turning and leaving the shop. There was no thank you or even a goodbye uttered.

Eliza released all the breath that she had been holding in during those last few minutes and sat down, defeated, on the stool behind the counter. Pupcake was at her feet, curled up with one of his back legs lifted off the floor. Eliza scooped down to pick him up and he nuzzled his tiny face against her neck.

What am I thinking, entering this contest? Eliza asked herself.

With her free hand, she pulled her phone out of her back pocket and called Dean to tell him everything.

After all the chicken and most of the potato salad and veggies were consumed, Dean opened a new bottle of wine filling everyone's glasses. Jason began laying out the dominos face down on the table in front of them.

"I keep meaning to ask you guys if your oven is working again?" Eliza was referring to a conversation she had with Susan a couple of weeks prior. Susan had asked to use the shop after hours to bake a casserole. Her oven had stopped working and she was expecting her in-laws the next day.

"What?" Jason asked, seeming confused.

"It's fine," Susan snapped, glaring at her husband.

Jason returned the stare, and tension hung in the air, as the two remained in that pose for what felt to Eliza like an uncomfortable amount of time. She assumed that the in-law visit must not have gone very well, and she glanced over at Dean, pleading with her eyes for him to change the subject.

"Anyone want anything?" Dean said, rising to his feet. "Water? I think I could use some water."

"Oh, me, too," Eliza said gratefully. "I'll take a glass of water."

Eliza began pulling her pile of dominos and setting them up in front of her, and she was relieved to see everyone follow suit. She hoped that whatever tough subject she had accidentally brought up had been swept under the rug for now.

"How are things going with the coffee shop, Eliza?" Jason asked. He glanced over quickly at his wife, and Eliza wondered if Susan had asked Jason not to discuss Eliza's coffee shop.

"Really great!" Eliza answered with genuine enthusiasm, also keeping an eye on Susan. She was quietly straightening up the dominos that Jason had placed on the table, separating them into two draw piles.

"Did you hear that Eliza is entering the county fair's baking contest?" Dean chimed in, throwing a smile and a wink over at Eliza.

Susan interjected and answered, "I did hear about that, actually. You probably don't know this, Eliza, but I joined the tennis club recently. You and your shop are quite the topic of discussion there, for some reason."

"Really?!" Eliza asked, sincerely surprised. "I didn't realize you played tennis, Sue."

Susan scoffed. "Yeah, well, it seems like you honestly don't know much about me anymore now that you're all caught up with your business."

Dean quickly defended his wife. "Well, that's hardly a fair statement, Susan. Eliza and you have been friends for years."

Susan cast a glance at Jason as if she wanted him to jump into the conversation, but Jason avoided eye contact and took a small sip of his wine.

Eliza reached over and gently touched Susan's arm. "I'm so happy for you to have found something you like to do, Sue. Tell me about it. How often do you play? Are you taking lessons?"

Susan pulled away and responded quietly, "Yeah, I'm taking lessons, and I'm making new friends."

Jason interrupted his wife, "Are we ready to play or what?"

Eliza and Dean both glanced at Susan with loving and concerned expressions. The interruption didn't go unnoticed and the tension in the room instantly became very thick. Susan stood and retrieved the open bottle of wine from the counter where Dean had left it, refilling her glass to the very top. She quickly gulped half of it down.

What is happening? thought Eliza. Susan was clearly in a much worse state than she had expected.

Pupcake woke and stretched into a downward dog position before planting his butt on the floor next to Eliza's chair. She bent at the waist and scooped him up with one hand, placing him in her lap.

"Pupcake wants to play, too," she chuckled. She had hoped that bringing everyone's attention to his cute little face might lighten the mood.

But she was wrong. Jason seemed to want to continue to challenge his wife. "Are we going to need more wine, Susan? Is it going to be one of those nights again?"

Dean and Eliza remained silent and wide-eyed, stunned by what was unfolding in front of them. Pupcake's ears twitched slightly as his eyes drifted back and forth from Jason to Susan's faces across the table. Eliza stroked Pupcake's fur from his neck to the base of his tail.

Susan guzzled the rest of her wine and set her wine glass down on the table, clearly upset with Jason's insensitive comment.

"So, now you're going to pretend that I have a drinking problem? What else, Jason? Looking for another excuse to walk away, I guess?"

Eliza couldn't tell if it was the wine or the emotion that was causing Susan's words to slur, and she fought the urge to interject.

"That's enough," Jason snapped. "I'm not doing this. I'm not going to sit here and put up with this." He jumped up, sending his chair backward a couple of feet and headed out the front door.

Pupcake grumbled quietly, disapproving of the noise level, and Eliza held him closer to her chest. She looked to Dean as if to plead with him to *Do something*.

On his way out of the room, Jason stopped and turned back to his wife, his eyes filled with emotion.

"Find a ride home. Or don't come home. I don't even care."

Dean rose from his seat and quickly followed Jason out the front door. Pupcake fidgeted in Eliza's lap, but she continued to hold the pup snugly against her chest.

Susan began crying and laid her head down on the table.

"I hate my life, Eliza," she muttered. "I really do."

Hearing the door shut, Eliza set Pupcake down on the floor and stood to comfort her long-time friend. Eliza hugged Susan and mustered kind and supportive words.

"It's ok, Sue. You'll get through this. Everything is going to be ok." Eliza desperately hoped that her state of shock was hidden in her voice. She had never seen her close friends speak to each other like this, and she felt helpless.

Moments later, Dean came back into the house without Jason.

With a quiet voice, full of concern, he explained, "Jason's pretty mad, but he said he would see you at home. I'm happy to drive you home if you'd like, whenever you're ready, Susan. I'm so sorry y'all are going through this."

Susan didn't lift her head. Her shoulders trembled rhythmically with each quiet sob that escaped. Eliza and Dean's eyes met. They were worried for their friends.

"I'll take care of her, Dean," Eliza said in a low voice. "Why don't you go on upstairs and get ready for bed?"

Dean nodded and gave his wife a look of gratitude. He hugged her tight and kissed her on the cheek before heading upstairs to relax.

Eliza stood. "I'm going to make you a cup of tea," she told her friend.

Eliza thought she heard Susan whisper, "Thank you," but she couldn't be sure.

Pupcake was lying on his bed by the back door but he was no longer asleep. He blinked his brown eyes at Eliza from across the kitchen.

Susan finally raised her head and rested on her hands, elbows set firmly on the table.

"Can we just take a girls' trip and get away for like a week or two, Eliza?" She used one of the cloth napkins thrown on the table after dinner to wipe underneath her eyes.

Eliza sighed. "I'm so sorry, Sue, but I can't take time away from the shop right now, and with the upcoming contest..." Her words trailed off.

"That's ok, Eliza. I already knew the answer," Susan responded.

She laid her head back down on the table, and Eliza's heart sank.

Canceled?

Eliza woke up early after a restless night of sleep. She was worried about Susan and struggled to push the incident from the previous night out of her mind. She sat on the edge of her bed and stretched her arms toward the sky before quietly tiptoeing to the bathroom, hoping not to disturb Dean who had another hour or more before his alarm.

She locked eyes with her reflection in the mirror, not surprised that she looked as tired as she felt.

Eliza's mind drifted, her toothbrush gliding back and forth over her teeth. She remembered fondly how just two years ago, the house would be bustling with energy in the early mornings. Eliza would start her day preparing a big breakfast for Dean and the kids, soaking up the happiness and laughter that filled the air. Happy and carefree was a great way to describe her life then. She missed it.

She realized that Susan also longed for that previous life. The two of them would chat on the phone every day. They would sometimes visit the grocery store together, grab lunch out or spend the afternoon at one or the others' houses playing Rummikub. Life was simple. They were all happier, especially Susan and Jason... or so she thought.

Eliza patted her face dry on the hand towel and forced a smile in the mirror. Things were different now, and not all bad. She had worked hard in therapy over the past couple of years to cherish the past with positive energy from the present, so she shifted her focus away from her friend's troubles and onto her busy schedule of the day.

She wrapped her hair into a messy bun at the nape of her neck and turned off the light before opening the door to the bedroom. Using the glow from her Apple watch, she grabbed the outfit she had laid out on the chair and quickly changed out of her pajamas. She smiled as she saw Pupcake sitting quietly in his playpen, slowly licking his paws. He was such a sweet, patient pup.

"Good morning," Dean mumbled.

"Oh, hi, sweetie. I'm so sorry I woke you." Eliza leaned over the side of the bed and gave Dean a kiss.

"It's okay," Dean said. "I'm glad you did. I have a busy day today." Running his hands through his hair and rubbing the light stubble that had grown overnight, he groaned quietly as he planted his feet on the floor.

Dean rose to his feet and headed toward the bathroom, stopping to squeeze his wife's shoulders and pet Pupcake who was now in her arms getting all kinds of kisses.

"I'm going to jump in the shower," he mumbled in Eliza's ear.

Eliza looked up from where she was nuzzling her face in Pupcake's soft neck fur and smiled at her husband.

"Okay, I'll start a pot of coffee and see you downstairs when you're finished."

She headed downstairs, carrying Pupcake as if he were a baby, his chin resting on her shoulder and her hand firmly on his back against her chest.

"You're such a big boy," she told Pupcake. It was a routine they had each morning, a sort of private joke between the two of them, where she told the tiny guy that he looked like he had grown overnight. Pupcake turned his head and licked Eliza a few times on the cheek as his tail wagged quickly back and forth.

She opened the door to the backyard and Pupcake sauntered outside. He was in no hurry and looked around as he peed in his favorite spot, making sure everything was still in place from the last time he was outside, and watching for birds and squirrels.

After starting a pot of coffee, Eliza settled down at the table, opening her laptop in front of her. It was time to place an order from her paper goods supplier. She had sent the inventory list to her personal email from the shop to make it easy.

She clicked on her inbox and waited as the new emails loaded and appeared one by one.

She gasped.

Right there, front and center was an email with the subject line: *Cancellation Confirmation*. The sender was listed as the Stillson County Fair Coordinator.

What now? Eliza thought. She didn't cancel! She clicked on the email and found a short note confirming that the county fair coordinator had received her request to not participate in the baking contest. Eliza slammed the laptop shut and ran upstairs to tell Dean, Pupcake in tow, following dangerously close to her feet.

Dean had just stepped out of the shower and was getting dressed when Eliza and Pupcake burst into the room. She filled Dean in on what she had just read.

"Who could do this to me?" Eliza was pacing. She had never faced such adversity before, and she truly didn't know how to deal with it.

"I don't know, honey. Let's think about this for a minute." Dean was standing in front of their full-length mirror, straightening his tie.

"Who is your competition?"

The minute he asked the question, Eliza stopped in her tracks.

"That's it! It's Margaret Minks that is doing this to me!"

"Wait - who is Margaret Minks again?"

"She's the mean lady I told you about who came into my shop the other day and threatened me." Eliza's words were mixed with anger and fear.

"Okay, hold on. When you called me the other day, you didn't say she *threatened* you," said Dean. "You said she told you that she always wins and that it would be a waste of time for you to enter the contest. And that she had bought a cupcake. That's not a threat."

"Well, it basically was a threat," Eliza insisted. "She was *not* friendly at all. I think she broke my window! Should we call the police?"

Dean sighed and turned to face his wife. He reached out and took her hands into his.

"I think we need to be very careful before we go around accusing someone of vandalism, and now corruption, too."

He squeezed Eliza's hands gently and spoke slowly. "I guess we could call the officer and tell him about her visit, but let's be careful to tell him only exactly what she said. We don't want to embellish the story. Let *him* do the investigation, if he decides to do so."

He released Eliza's hands to reach down and pick up Pupcake, who sat on the floor with his left foot lifted.

"First things first, though, my love. You need to reach out to the county fair coordinator and let her know that you didn't cancel and that you still want to compete."

Eliza nodded. Her stomach filled with dread.

"I don't know now, Dean, if I should even do this. Running my shop was fun and wonderful until I entered this stupid contest. I hate that it has turned into this."

Dean shifted Pupcake to his side and embraced Eliza in a warm hug with his free arm.

"Eliza, I will support you, no matter what you decide to do. But you faced your fears to get this far with your shop, and it has paid off. Big time. There is always going to be another challenge ahead of you in life, and I want you to feel as if you're strong enough to tackle anything - because you can.

Even if you don't win this baking contest, you'll be proud of yourself for trying and there will only be positive things that can come as a result of that."

Eliza sighed, exhaling slowly and returned the warm hug, squeezing her husband tight against her body, her hands wrapped around his waist.

"Thank you, Dean," she mumbled, her face buried in his chest. "I know you're right."

She pulled back and pressed her lips against his, falling in love with him all over again.

"You've gotten quite good at these pep talks, you know that?"

"I've been taking notes all these years. These are all things you've said to our kids, and they're happy, healthy and living awesome lives right now."

Dean leaned in for another kiss and Eliza's nerves settled as she was filled with warmth.

"Now go send that email. I'm gonna pour us each a cup of coffee, and then we'll call the officer and fill him in on everything together."

The Deadline

E liza and Pupcake arrived at the shop extra early. Her cupcakes were due for the baking contest later that afternoon, and she wanted to make sure she had enough time to get laser-focused on making everything perfect before she opened for the day. She had double-checked to make sure she had all the ingredients before she left the night before but went through the list one by one again. Triple-checking the list brought a welcome calm to her anxious mood.

She settled Pupcake in with his bed, blanket and water bowl, poured fresh water into the coffee carafe and pushed it into place in the old-school coffee maker. Normally, she would prepare a chai latte for herself, but today, she needed a good ol' cup of Joe. Resting for a few minutes on the stool behind the counter, waiting for the coffee to brew, Eliza took a few slow deep breaths and watched as Pupcake nested his blanket into another perfect circle. The past few days and weeks had been such a whirlwind, but Eliza suspected things would settle down after her cupcakes were safely submitted into the fair's contest.

With perfect timing, Eliza's phone chimed. She had received a text message from Taylor stating she would not be coming into work because of a migraine headache.

Are you kidding me? Eliza said out loud, shaking her head. She couldn't help but wonder if Taylor was working with her aunt to once again try to sabotage her chance of winning.

The officer said that he did not have enough evidence to arrest Margaret Minks for the vandalism and that she was pretty convincing with an alibi for that early morning. The case was still open and being investigated, but there were no leads.

There was also no evidence that Margaret had tried to sabotage Eliza's entry in the contest. Luckily, the county fair coordinator had responded quickly to Eliza when she wrote to explain that she had not submitted a cancellation and wanted to be reinstated back into the running.

Her cupcakes were officially back in the contest, and Eliza was eager to meet the coordinator in person and try to get to the bottom of what could've happened. She hoped that in the end, she would find out that it was just a clerical mistake and not some kind of personal vendetta.

Eliza responded to Taylor's text with a thumbs up emoji and a short message that read, "I hope you feel better soon."

Eliza rubbed her face with her hands and cleared her thoughts of all the negativity for now. She needed to be focused on creating the perfect strawberry cream cheese cupcakes instead.

"It's just you and me today, Pupcake," she said, as she stood to her feet. Pupcake, now comfortable in his bed, met her gaze and blinked twice as if to say, *We got this, Mom,* and Eliza grinned.

Her excitement around the prospect of being featured in the *Sugar and Spice* magazine had returned as she donned a clean apron. An avid reader of that magazine for years, there was no denying that a prize like that would be a dream come true for Eliza and Pupcake's Corner Café.

She set to work, carefully measuring and mixing the ingredients one by one. The cupcake batter was perfectly delicious, and Eliza knew again that Dean was right. Even if she didn't win the blue ribbon, it was still a great experience, throwing her hat in the ring with her most popular item.

Eliza placed the cupcakes in the oven and set the timer for a few minutes earlier than normal to ensure she didn't overbake them. Then, she shifted her focus to creating the cream cheese icing and washing and slicing the strawberries, setting both in the cooler as she finished. The timer started beeping as she was filling her cash register with the day's change.

Throughout the remainder of the morning, Eliza's mood was lifted as she held lively conversations with the customers. Everyone was friendly and understanding of her being short-staffed. It helped that Pupcake was there to entertain each customer with his cuteness. As busy as it was, Eliza kept one eye on the clock to make sure she allowed herself enough time to travel the 45 minutes to the conference center. The contest required that all baked goods be submitted between the hours of three and five that afternoon. The judging was set to begin an hour after the deadline, at six, and the winners were to be announced the very next day at the fair's baking exhibit.

As two o'clock rolled around, with just an hour until the opening of the drop-off times, Pupcake's Corner Café was empty. Eliza locked the door and flipped the sign over to show the shop was closed. She carefully decorated each cupcake, ecstatic about how beautiful they looked when she had finished. She packed up the decorated cupcakes and checked two more times to make sure that the cover of the box was intact and secured tightly.

Eliza hung her apron on a wall hook and slipped Pupcake into his sling, already hanging around her neck. She then grabbed her purse and keys with one hand and balanced the box of cupcakes in her other hand. She exited the back door and locked it securely.

She pressed the clicker on her keyring to unlock her car doors and tried to open the hatchback. It was locked, so she pushed the clicker again.

Still nothing. The door was still locked.

Eliza set the box of cupcakes on top of the car and opened the hatch with the key. She set the cupcakes in the back of her car where they would be safest from the outside warm temperatures and most secure from movement. Closing the hatchback, she unlocked the driver's side door next and climbed inside. She unzipped the sling pocket and Pupcake climbed into his seat in the passenger seat. She clicked the buckle on his seat belt and threw the sling in the backseat.

She took a deep breath and slipped the key in the ignition.

"Okay, let's do this," she said to Pupcake. He responded with a tail wag before settling into the seated position.

She turned the key. There was a clicking sound, but then the car fell silent.

She tried again.

Oh no, thought Eliza. She fished her phone out of her pocket and quickly called her husband. There was no answer, and Eliza disconnected the call just as the familiar voicemail message began. She called Dean's office, and his assistant reminded her that he had to be in court that afternoon.

Eliza couldn't believe this was happening. What a roller coaster this entire experience had been. She brushed away the thoughts of just giving up on the whole contest and gave Susan a call. Again, she was met with voicemail. She hit the end button and sent Susan a text message instead. She waited a few seconds, but there was no response.

Pupcake looked over at Eliza and whimpered softly.

"I don't know what's happening," Eliza said out loud, her voice cracking as she fought back tears.

Fighting the feeling of panic setting in, she called Jason next. He answered on the second ring.

"What's happening? Is everything ok?" It was strange for Eliza to call Jason, and he was immediately worried when he saw her name pop up on his phone.

"Hi, Jason!" Elza continued to push back tears and cleared her throat before continuing. "I'm at the shop and I have to get to the fair in Manson before 5:00, and my car suddenly won't start."

"Dean is in court, and Susan won't answer her phone," she explained, the words rushing out of her mouth faster than a runaway train.

"I'll be right there," Jason responded. Eliza suspected he sensed the urgency in her voice.

Within ten minutes, Jason arrived in his truck. Eliza had pulled herself together and was standing by her car, holding the cupcakes. Pupcake was back in his sling.

"Jump in!" Jason said after he rolled down his window.

"Are you sure? Don't you want to see if you can fix my car first? It's a forty-minute drive or so, you know." Eliza asked.

"No worries. I'll just drive you so we aren't late. I'll look at the car when we get back." Jason smiled, reached over, and pushed the passenger door open.

"Thank you so much, Jason. You're a lifesaver!" Eliza and Pupcake climbed into Jason's truck. She carefully opened the pastry box to check on her cupcakes. All was in order.

It's Not Just Business

Eliza, Pupcake, and Jason made it to the conference center with plenty of time to spare. Jason offered to hang out with Pupcake, and Eliza took him up on the offer. She had not considered what she was going to do with him if there was a no-dogs-allowed policy in the building.

Walking in, Eliza proudly held the light blue striped box that held her cupcakes. She was confident they still looked just as beautiful as when she had made them a few hours earlier, and there was no doubt they tasted just as good as they looked. She followed the signs to the table where contestants were to sign in and turn in their baked goods. Joining the long line, a voice that she recognized drifted her way.

A bead of sweat accumulated on the back of Eliza's neck as she realized it was Margaret Minks' voice she was hearing, and that her biggest competitor was only a few steps ahead of her in line. Leaning toward the side, she could see that only one woman stood in line between the two of them. She switched the box from her right hand to her left hand, wiping her clammy right hand on her hip as she waited her turn. She focused on quietly breathing in and out slowly. She didn't want to come face to face with Margaret. Not today, and certainly not after everything she had been through the past few weeks.

"Welcome, Margaret! Are you back to claim the winning prize again this year, I guess?" A judge chuckled as she spoke to Margaret as if they were old friends.

"I do expect to win. My apple pie has held the title for the last seven years. I can't imagine not winning, honestly, and I can't wait to meet the editors of *Sugar and Spice*." Margaret sounded much more friendly here than she had when she visited the Pupcake's Corner Café.

"Well, you know the drill. Leave it with us, sign right here, and then we'll announce the winners tomorrow night at the exhibit." The judge pushed the piece of paper towards Margaret. After Margaret signed the paper, the judge winked at her and said, "Good luck! We'll see you tomorrow!"

Eliza couldn't help but notice that the shoulders of the lady who stood between her and Margaret drooped a little, but she stepped forward and softly announced her name before presenting her platter of expertly decorated cookies.

She signed the paper and walked away, looking relieved. Eliza wondered how hard that woman had worked to get her cookies here on time.

It was Eliza's turn next. "Hi," the judge greeted her with a broad smile. "What is your name, please?"

"Eliza Campbell. I'm here with my strawberry cream cheese cupcakes." Eliza remembered telling her daughter to stand up tall with her shoulders pushed back whenever she wasn't feeling confident, and she put that same thing into practice as she stood before the judge.

The judge reached for the box and passed it to the lady who was helping assist her with the check-ins. She peeked inside and said, "Oh, those look yummy! Thank you for your submission! Now, if you'll just sign right here, you'll be all set." She passed the paper to Eliza. Eliza signed the paper, embracing a sense of relief that she had finally submitted her cupcakes and was near the end of the process.

"Oh, one more thing, please," Eliza remembered, "Can I please speak to the county fair coordinator? She is expecting me."

The judge directed her to a small office and Eliza headed in that direction. Eliza walked in and introduced herself to the lady sitting behind the desk.

"Hi, my name is Eliza Campbell, and I'm here about the cancellation that was submitted."

The lady pressed her lips together in a slight smile and returned the greeting.

"Hi, I'm Betty Cohen. I'm glad you made it in today," she said with a professional tone and a friendly nod.

"Thank you so much for reversing that cancellation for me. I'm still just so confused how that could have happened. I wanted to ask if you know anything else about how a cancellation request could have been submitted for my entry in the baking contest?" Eliza placed her hands in her pockets, hoping to hide any signs of nervous anxiety.

"Oh right, yeah, that was odd. Someone called me and said she was you, and that you weren't well. That you needed to cancel. She verified your information - your phone number, your address, your email address, your submission type... so I had no other reason but to assume it was you calling. I'm so sorry about that confusion. I agree that *is* strange. I've never experienced anything like that in all the years I've been doing this."

Eliza felt like someone had punched her in the gut. The person who was trying to sabotage her was someone close enough to know all of her information.

She swallowed hard and thanked the coordinator, promising to see her tomorrow at the exhibit.

Exiting the building, she found Jason and Pupcake right outside waiting for her. She scooped up Pupcake and grabbed Jason by the arm, leading the way to where his truck was parked.

"Oh my gosh, Jason. You'll never believe this…"

As they began the drive back to Copeland, she proceeded to tell Jason everything that had happened in the previous two weeks.

"So, the coordinator said someone called in, and they had all my information! There's no way that Margaret Minks would know all of that. Maybe she could have figured out my home address and phone number, but I used my personal email address to register, not my business email address. I can't imagine how she would have known that."

"It just doesn't make sense…" Jason said, stumped, but intrigued.

"All I know," Eliza said, "is that this was personal." She petted Pupcake behind the ears as she struggled emotionally with what she knew to be the truth.

Friend or Foe?

On the way back to the shop, Eliza called Susan again. This time, Susan answered the phone.

"What, Eliza?" Susan snapped before Eliza had a chance to say anything.

"Susan. Tell me you didn't try to sabotage the baking contest for me." Eliza got right to the point.

"What are you talking about, Eliza? Why would I try to sabotage your little baking contest?" Susan responded, her voice loaded with contempt.

"That's what I'm trying to figure out. I can't wrap my head around the idea that someone I've known and loved all these years would do something so mean." Eliza was fighting tears, looking out the passenger window.

Jason shifted in the driver's seat, clearly uncomfortable with what he was hearing. He knew his wife, Susan, was struggling with things, and she had been complaining to him about Eliza a lot lately.

But, from the sound of it, Susan had done some pretty horrible things to her friend, and he was worried that their relationship might be in real trouble.

"Maybe you should be less self-absorbed in that stupid little coffee shop and your stupid baking contest. I don't even know who you are anymore." Susan snapped.

Eliza gasped. Was Susan actually admitting that she was behind all of this?

"Susan, tell me you did not break my shop's window."

Susan was silent.

Eliza's head was spinning. It was all becoming clear now.

Her personal information was provided to the fair co-ordinator. Of course, that was what led Eliza to Susan eventually.

The brick was thrown in the window. The threat was written using the blue pen and the paper from Pupcake's Corner Cafe. Eliza now remembered that she had given Susan a copy of the key and the alarm code when she first opened the shop. Susan had asked to use the kitchen after hours when her oven suddenly stopped working, and she was expecting a visit from her in-laws the next day.

Susan had not returned the key, and Eliza remembered now how Susan quickly interrupted and talked over her that night at dinner when she asked if her oven had been fixed.

Pupcake acted so strangely around Susan that night, too, Eliza remembered. He must have somehow sensed her ill intent and was trying to warn Eliza about her old friend.

Eliza was instantly ashamed that she hadn't put the pieces together sooner.

"Susan! How could you do all of this to me?" Eliza shrieked into the phone, unable to hide her frustration and hurt.

"What do you mean, how could I do all of this to *you*? You have completely deserted me, Eliza. All you care about is your coffee shop. Nothing else matters to you." Susan broke into sobs.

"That's not true, Susan. I'm sorry you are having such a hard time, but these things you did... I didn't deserve any of that." A tear sped down Eliza's cheek, and she wiped it away with the back of her hand.

Pupcake fidgeted in his safety seat, situated between Eliza and Jason, itching to get out and comfort his person.

After a moment of quiet, Susan's tone changed.

"I'm so sorry, Eliza. Please forgive me. I don't know what I'd do without you in my life." Susan sobbed. "I'll make it right. I promise!"

Susan continued to cry and speak, but the phone was losing service and Eliza couldn't make out what her old friend was saying. The call disconnected.

A sense of relief washed over Eliza. She needed some time to decide if she was going to be able to get past everything her best friend had done to her.

"I hope you know that I didn't know about any of this, Eliza," Jason said after a moment of quiet. You could almost feel the tension in the air.

"I know," Eliza said, sounding defeated.

"I do know that Susan loves you dearly," he continued. "She hasn't been herself lately, but she needs you in her life." He glanced over at Eliza who had returned to petting Pupcake.

Once they had returned to the shop, Jason quickly determined that the battery cables in Eliza's car had simply been disconnected. He was able to reconnect the cables in no time at all, and Eliza and Pupcake were on their way home within minutes.

All Eliza wanted was to tell Dean everything, his arms wrapped around her in one of those signature hugs that made her feel so safe. He would know what to say.

And the Winner Is...

The county fair was alive with energy. Tables were set up along the front and sides of the tent, covered in beautifully decorated baked goods of all kinds. Men, women and children were all standing shoulder to shoulder, facing the stage in the front, filled with anticipation for the winner announcements. Eliza and Dean stood a few rows back from the stage. Dean was wearing Pupcake's sling. Eliza always chuckled when she saw Dean's broad shoulders and tall figure wearing the sling, which resembled a purse, with only Pupcake's tiny head sticking out, tongue wagging. The two of them were the cutest duo ever.

Dean insisted on wearing the sling today so that Eliza "could be free to accept her ribbon." She had blushed when he said it, but if she were being honest, she thought she had a pretty good chance of at least winning the second or third prize.

A woman wearing a large-brimmed hat stood near the very front of the crowd, close to the steps to the stage. She turned her head slightly, and Eliza immediately recognized her face. It was Margaret Minks. *She's poised as if she's ready to step onto the stage*, Eliza thought, as her confidence dropped a couple of notches.

There were five women on the stage. The woman wearing a floral patterned knee-length dress was the lady that Eliza had spoken to the day before when she dropped off her cupcakes. She was the county fair coordinator. She stepped up to the wooden podium and tapped the microphone a few times to test the sound. A quiet hush fell over the crowd and a heightened excited tension filled the air.

Eliza leaned in close to Pupcake's face so that she could receive a quick kiss on the cheek. Her stomach was in knots from nerves, and a little kiss from Pupcake always helped with that.

The coordinator smiled as she spoke with a clear, loud voice. "Thank you for coming today. My name is Betty Cohen, and I am this year's county fair coordinator. I would like to start by saying a very special thank you to all you wonderful bakers who submitted your delicious treats in Stillson County's 12th Annual Baking contest. It was a very tough decision this year, I'll tell ya."

One of the other ladies on stage sneaked a wave and a wink directed at Margaret. Eliza stifled a gasp and exchanged quick glances with Dean. He leaned over and whispered, "You got this, babe" with a big smile and a quick wink of his own. Eliza smiled back and nodded.

Turning her shoulders a bit, Betty reached her right arm out to gracefully point out three of the remaining ladies on the stage. Each of the ladies was middle-aged or older, dressed in their Sunday's finest dresses and smiling from ear to ear. "I would like to introduce our judges, Emily Mass, Stefanie Boulder, and Amy Strauss. These gracious ladies are all certified as county fair culinary judges, and they have had the great pleasure of tasting each and every dessert that you see on our tables today. Let's please give them a round of applause."

The sound of clapping mixed with a few whistles and enthusiastic hoots and hollers rose above the crowd. Eliza instinctively glanced over at Pupcake to make sure he was okay with the noise, and he seemed fine. His eyes focused forward toward the stage as if he were also anticipating the winner announcements.

Once the cheering died down, Betty swiveled and reached her left hand out in the other direction, pointing to the woman on stage wearing a very professional-looking pale yellow suit dress. She continued, "And last, but certainly not least, I have the great pleasure of introducing our special guest, Sharon McArthur, the editor of the renowned *Sugar and Spice* magazine."

Betty didn't have to ask for a round of applause for Sharon. Everyone was familiar with the *Sugar and Spice* magazine, and the crowd was more than excited to see Ms. McArthur on the stage.

After a few moments, Betty raised her hand to show that it was time to move on and for the cheering to subside for now. She cleared her throat. "Today, we will announce three winners. Third Place will receive the white ribbon and a $50 cash prize. The second-place winner will receive the red ribbon and a $100 cash prize. The Grand Prize, the First Place winner will receive the coveted blue ribbon, a $500 cash prize and a feature in next month's *Sugar and Spice* magazine edition!"

The crowd erupted once again. Betty smiled and clapped along, turning back to throw another glance of recognition toward Sharon McArthur who smiled and clapped, as well.

Eliza grabbed Dean's hand and squeezed it tight. Her anxiety was building, her stomach filled with fluttering butterflies. Dean looked at her and smiled, his free hand petting Pupcake's head. Eliza smiled back and edged in as close as she could to her husband and Pupcake.

It was time for the winners to be announced.

Betty held up the white ribbon and continued, "The White Ribbon of the Stillson County Fair's 12th Annual Baking contest goes to Allison Irwin for her German chocolate cake. Congratulations, Allison, c'mon up and collect your prize!" The tent was filled with applause again as a young lady who looked to be in her mid-twenties bounded up the steps to the stage and shook Betty's hand while the event photographer grabbed a quick photo opportunity.

After the young lady returned to her spot in the crowd and received lots of pats on the backs and friendly congratulations from everyone around her, Betty continued. "The Stillson County Fair's 12th Annual Baking Contest's Red Ribbon goes to Margaret Minks for her apple pie. Congratulations, Margaret!"

Eliza gasped. Margaret won second place!

She found herself filled with mixed emotions. Seeing Margaret's forced smile on stage, posing for her picture, she could tell that Margaret was disappointed. Eliza felt a tug on her heart. So much work went into preparing for this contest, and she knew Margaret thought she would win again this year.

On the other hand, Eliza couldn't help but feel excited, realizing that Margaret did *not* win the first prize. She could still win this! She took a deep breath. Dean released her hand and wrapped his arm around her shoulders instead, and Eliza leaned into the embrace, grabbing onto Pupcake with her right hand.

"I am so excited to announce the winner of the Grand Prize!" Betty squealed with excitement before continuing, "The Stillson County Fair's 12th Annual Baking Contest's First Place Blue Ribbon goes to Eliza Campbell for her delicious, and beautiful strawberry cream cheese cupcakes! Congratulations, Eliza! C'mon up here!"

Eliza let out a scream just before her hands covered her mouth. She jumped up and down and threw her arms around Dean's neck, kissing him and Pupcake before she headed up to the stage. She passed Margaret Minks on the way, but Margaret was headed in the opposite direction. She accepted the blue ribbon and the check and then turned to shake hands with Betty, all three judges and Sharon McArthur, posing for picture after picture along the way.

Eliza felt like she was dreaming. Dean was right. It was an incredible feeling to push through obstacles and face a challenge.

She couldn't wait to hang the blue ribbon in Pupcake's Corner Café - she had already decided just where to put it, and she would be sure to save room for the framed article that was soon to follow.

Sharon McArthur from the *Sugar & Spice* magazine caught up to Eliza as she, Dean and Pupcake were headed to their car to leave.

"Eliza!" Sharon called out. "I just wanted to say congratulations again. I'm serious, those cupcakes are incredible! I have heard great things about your cafe in Copeland. I was wondering if I could come by there and conduct the interview and take photos for the magazine on location. What do you think?"

"Oh my gosh, yes," Eliza exclaimed. "I would love that!" She introduced Dean to Sharon. "Sharon, this is my husband, Dean. He's the reason I have Pupcake's Corner Café at all."

Dean shook hands with Sharon and said, "Hi, Sharon. I'm Eliza's biggest fan, but she's built that place into the success that it is today, all on her own."

Sharon smiled, but she was distracted by the super cute pup in the sling across Dean's chest.

"And tell me," Sharon continued, "Is this *the* Pupcake that the cafe is named for?" She reached out to pet Pupcake's head and he leaned into it, his eyes only half-open.

"The one and only," Eliza said with a grin. "Ahh… he really likes you. I have always said he's a good judge of character."

A New Name

Taylor placed three coffee cups on the front counter.

"I think I made them just the way everyone likes them," she said. "Susan, yours is on the end there." She pointed to the cup on the far right.

"Oh, thank you," Susan said. She picked up the cup and took a sip. "It's perfect!"

Eliza came around the corner from the kitchen and grabbed the cup from the center.

"Taylor makes the best coffee," she said, thanking her as well.

"Susan, it is so nice to have her here, I have to say," Taylor said. "It makes the morning rush much easier."

"Agreed," Eliza said, winking at Susan. "You are a life-saver, honestly."

Susan blushed. "Well, I'm the one who is grateful to be here. I love getting to spend time with my best friend again, and I had no idea how much I would look forward to this every day!"

Pupcake came sauntering around the corner of the front counter and sat at Susan's feet, his left back foot lifted off the ground.

"Oh, come here, you sweet thing," Susan said as she bent down to pick him up and cuddle him.

"You have no idea how glad I am to see that the two of you have made up," Eliza joked.

Susan chuckled. "Yeah, I think he forgives me for all the crazy stuff I've done," she said. Then, looking at Eliza, she said, "And I'm so glad that you were able to forgive me, too." Eliza thought Susan's eyes misted a bit before looking back at Pupcake.

"Me too," Eliza said. "I just can't imagine life without you."

With much encouragement from Dean and after a long tearful conversation with Susan, Eliza had been able to move forward with her twenty-plus year friendship and put everything that had happened into the past. Susan and Jason's marriage had not been able to recover in the same way, however, and they had decided on an amicable divorce. Eliza needed another pair of hands at the cafe, and Susan needed a healthy distraction, so her addition to the Pupcake Corner Cafe team was a win-win for everyone.

Right on time, the front door opened, and Mrs. Wilson walked in wearing a smile that spread from ear to ear.

"Good morning, Mrs. Wilson!" Susan greeted her warmly from behind the counter.

"Good morning, Susan! Will I see you on Tuesday for the women's league this week?" Mrs. Wilson responded.

"Oh, not this week. Things have picked up here at the shop, and I'll be working more hours with Eliza." Susan and Eliza exchanged smiles.

Eliza chimed in, "I'm sorry to steal one of your players, but I just don't know how I ever got along without Susan, Mrs. Wilson! She is such a tremendous help around here."

She pushed the lid onto the disposable cup filled with hot chai tea latte as Susan packaged Mrs. Wilson's cheese danish in a blue striped cardboard box, wrapped a string of twine around the box and tied a neat little bow on top.

Mrs. Wilson paid for her order and dropped a $5 bill in the tip jar.

"Well, I'm so glad to see business is booming. I'll catch up with you at the club when you can make it, Susan. Thank you, ladies! Have a wonderful day!" Mrs. Wilson passed Margaret Minks on the way out and held the door open for her as Margaret entered the shop.

"Good morning, Margaret!" Eliza welcomed her new friend. Pupcake ran over to say hello, and Margaret waved at Eliza and bent down to give him a couple soft pats on the head.

Margaret rose to her feet and approached the counter. "Good morning."

"Can we get you anything today, Ms. Minks?" Susan asked politely.

Margaret shook her head. "No, thank you," she said with a shy smile. "I just wanted to check in to see how the apple pie has been selling."

Eliza interjected. "It's a huge hit! I was going to call you today and order more. We are down to less than two pies, and that won't be enough to get through the day. Our customers love it!

"Oh, and I wanted to show you something," Eliza said, pointing to the case.

Margaret's gaze followed where Eliza was pointing. Her smile grew, and she clasped her hands together. "You changed the name! I love it so much - thank you!"

Pupcake stood on his back feet next to Margaret and spun in a circle, picking up on the excitement.

Eliza grinned and nodded, "It only seemed fitting to call it what it is."

The food label card placed in front of the pie read, *7 Year Blue Ribbon Apple Pie.*

"Maybe next year, we'll have to change it to eight," Eliza winked.

———ℓℓℓ———

For an alternate ending filled with unexpected twists and deeper secrets, visit marybbarbee.com/pupcake-alternate -endings/to uncover how Eliza's story could have taken a different turn.

———ℓℓℓ———

Are you ready to read the next book in The Pupcake Mystery Series? In *Sweet Suspicion*, Eliza and Pupcake find themselves smack dab in the center of a murder investigation. As things start to heat up, Eliza and Pupcake must navigate through a maze of secrets and suspects to catch the killer before they strike again. But with the whole town on edge, can they trust anyone?

Grab your copy of the first book in The Pupcake Mystery Series at marybbarbee.com today, and get ready to sink your teeth into a deliciously suspenseful tale of murder, mystery, and fur-tastic sleuthing at the Pupcake Corner Café!

MARY B. BARBEE

About the Author

Mary B. Barbee is the author of the *Amish Lantern Mystery Series,* the *Abigail Baker Mystery Series, The Pupcake Mystery Series, and more.* As an avid fan of all mystery and suspense in print, on television and in film, Mary B. believes the best mystery is one where the suspect changes throughout the story, keeping the audience guessing. She enjoys providing an exciting escape for a few hours with stories her readers can't put down - and always with a surprise ending.

When not writing, Mary B. is either playing a couple sets of tennis or a strategy board game with her two witty daughters and her kindly competitive mother. The four of them share a home in the Inland Northwest in the beautiful town of Spokane, Washington with their really cute - but sometimes naughty - chihuahua.

Mary loves to hear from her readers. Connect at:
marybbarbee@gmail.com
www.facebook.com/marybbarbee
Instagram @marybbarbee
www.marybbarbee.com

More Books to Read
By Mary B. Barbee

THE AMISH LANTERN MYSTERY SERIES

Thick As Thieves – Book 1

Robberies are running rampant in Little Valley, and the quiet small-town lives of the Amish community are suddenly thrown into chaos.

Secrets in Little Valley – Book 2

With the bishop's daughter suddenly missing and a new sheriff in town, Anna and Beth find themselves roped into solving another mystery in their small town.

Saving Grace – Book 3

The Amish community in Little Valley is facing big changes, and big threats, with tourism booming. It becomes clear that some of the new businesses want control of the market, and it looks like they are willing to go to great lengths to get it.

Good Intentions – Book 4

Hazel Thompson is found dead in Little Valley's now-famous Amish Inn, and there's a long list of suspects with plenty of motive.

A Blessing in Disguise – Book 5

Jessica McLean opens shop to find a man has been left for dead on the floor of her diner. Could the crime could be related to Jessica's new relationship with their beloved Matthew Beiler?

Christmas Chaos in Little Valley - Book 6

Beth finds out that the Little Valley library is shutting its doors due to a lack of funding and very disturbing anonymous threats.

THE ABIGAIL BAKER MYSTERY SERIES
Blind Faith – Prequel

Abigail's excitement for her new home is replaced by doom and gloom when she finds out that an unexplained murder has rocked the residents of her new town. And not unusual to her, it's the Amish community that is suspect number one.

Grab your free e-copy of Blind Faith at:
marybbarbee.com/blindfaith

Where Fear Ends – Book 1

A town councilman is found dead by the side of the road in the Amish community of Abigail Baker's new hometown.

A Multitude of Sins – Book 2

When secret notes containing serious threats are unveiled, Abigail wonders if the latest victim could have been hiding a multitude of sins.

A Wing and a Prayer – Book 3 ~ COMING SOON!

THE PUPCAKE MYSTERY SERIES
Cupcakes and Corruption – Prequel

Battling empty-nest syndrome, Eliza finds solace in the company of her adorable chihuahua, Pupcake, and her dreams of opening a quaint coffee shop. Little does she know that her talent for baking and nurturing also extends to amateur sleuthing.

Grab your free e-copy of Cupcakes and Corruption at: marybbarbee.com/pupcakeprequel

Sweet Suspicion – Book 1

The charming town of Copeland is buzzing with excitement as Eliza and her adorable chihuahua, Pupcake, open their new coffee shop. But when a body is discovered on the premises, the duo must put down their baking tools and pick up their detective hats.

Confections and Clues – Book 2 – Coming Valentine's Day 2025

Eliza and Pupcake's lakeside getaway takes a dark turn when they stumble upon a body. With a secretive small town and a case no one wants solved, Eliza's sweet retreat quickly turns into another mystery. Can she and Pupcake crack the case before the killer's trail goes cold?

Recipe for Reckoning – Book 3 ~ COMING SOON!

Find excerpts, purchase links and more at

www.marybbarbee.com

www.ingramcontent.com/pod-product-compliance
Lightning Source LLC
Chambersburg PA
CBHW020618130626
46552CB00003B/1029